COLOUR JETS

HARRY FLY

Tasha Pym and Ken Cox

A&C Black • London

COLOUR JETS

Colour Me Crazy	Andrew Donkin
The Footprints Mystery	Andrew Donkin
Captain Skywriter and Kid Wonder	Stephen Elboz
Dad on the Run	Sarah Garland
Gertie and the Bloop	Julia Jarman
Stinker Muggles and the Dazzle Bug	Elizabeth Laird
Under the Red Elephant	Jan Mark
Francis Fry, Private Eye	Sam McBratney
Francis Fry and the O.T.G.	Sam McBratney
Sick As a Parrot	Michaela Morgan
Harry Fly	Tasha Pym
Aunt Jinksie's Miracle Seeds	Shoo Rayner
Boys Are Us	Shoo Rayner
Even Stevens F.C.	Michael Rosen
Dear Alien	Angie Sage
Reggie the Stuntman	Kate Shannon

For my dad

Published 1998 by A & C Black (Publishers) Ltd
35 Bedford Row, London WC1R 4JH

First published in paperback in Great Britain by
HarperCollins Publishers Ltd 1998

Text © Tasha Pym 1998
Illustrations © Ken Cox 1998

Tasha Pym and Ken Cox assert the moral right to be identified
as the author and the illustrator of the work.

A CIP record for this title is available from the British Library.

ISBN 0 7136 4915 1

Printed in Italy.

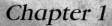

Chapter 1

Harry Fly narrowed his eyes and focused on the high jump bar ahead of him.

"This is it!" said a voice somewhere in his head. Harry's stomach lurched like an old washing machine. "Last chance to make the team!" said the voice.

Harry blinked, sucked in one last gulp of air, and…

…charged…

…sprang…

...flew...

...flew some more...

and...

Thwump!… landed on the crash mat. Harry opened one eye a crack. Way above him, the bar teetered on its ballasts. Reflecting the sun, it seemed to be winking at him.

I've done it! I've really done it!!

And Harry really thought that he had, until…

Mr Stebbings blew his whistle and Harry slunk, deflated, off to change.

7

Harry felt deflated for the rest of the day. *Why* was he so useless at high jump?

Fly's adopted, if you ask me.

Either that or a freak of nature, hur hur!

And *why* did Jason and Elvis have to sit behind him?!

At home time, Harry felt even worse.

Mum! Mum! I'm in the school team!

Me too!

Harry isn't.

"Oh dear, Harry," said Elvis's mum. "Whatever will you tell your parents?"

Harry shrugged. He hadn't quite worked that out yet.

As he walked off, Harry was sure that they were talking about him.

He decided that the best thing to do was tell his parents straight away, before anybody else did.

Chapter 2

Harry's biggest problem was that BOTH of his parents had won Gold Medals for High Jump at the Olympic Games.

Now they were well-known coaches.

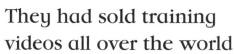

They had sold training videos all over the world

and they always, *always* wore their gold medals.

When Harry got home, Barbara and Harry Fly Senior were watching the video of the Olympic Games where they'd first met.

"Oh, well done," beamed his mum. "Was it easy-peasy?"

Eventually Harry gave up. After all, how *do* you tell your Olympic Gold Medal-winning parents that you can't even make the *school* team?

Chapter 3

Harry always went to The Gap when he wanted to be alone. Skimming stones across the lake helped him to think.

But with only two weeks to go before the inter-schools championship, *how…?*

Harry's ideas were just starting to get out of hand, when…

Hi, Harry!

It was Lucy Silver, the tallest person in the school – and one of the best high jumpers. Suddenly feeling very small, Harry sat down and threw another stone.

Lucy watched it skip into the distance.

Wow! You're a real ace!

I'm sorry you didn't make the team. It's tough being the smallest, I know.

How would you know?

"Because it's the same being the tallest," Lucy said, trying to skim a stone like Harry's. With a plop, it vanished. "And anyway," she added, "*you'll* grow!"

17

That night, Harry couldn't sleep. The day's events played over and over in his mind.

Finally, with Lucy's words ringing in his ears, his eyes grew heavy and closed.

Chapter 4

Almost the second Harry woke up, the idea came to him. He leapt out of bed (with the best jump he'd done that week) and hurried out of the house to get to school early.

Harry set to work

collecting the things

he would need.

By four o'clock, Harry had everything required to set his plan in motion.

And later that evening, when his parents were busy polishing their medals, Harry sneaked out to the garage.

A little later, Lucy walked down the Flys' driveway. As she passed the garage she heard a faint sound – a sort of muffled gasping.

Lucy pushed the side door open an inch. What she saw made *her* gasp.

Harry!

You said I'd grow. But I can't wait for time to make me grow, so I'm sort of stretching time, see?

Lucy was speechless. She didn't think it could possibly work, but she didn't dare say anything.

"They used to stretch people in the old days," Harry said, as if he was reading her mind. "And it worked then."

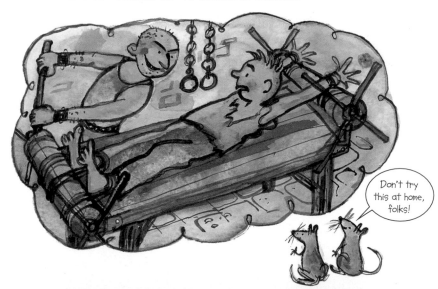

Don't try this at home, folks!

Chapter 5

Harry hung from the rafters every morning at dawn, and again every evening. In addition, he trained at The Gap after school.

Most days Lucy would come and take notes: comments, measurements – that sort of thing.

And every night, before he went to bed,
Harry recorded the results in a log book.

Nothing got in the way of Harry's training schedule. Not even the constant taunting from Jason and Elvis…

You're not normal, Fly.

Nope.

There's something going on.

Yup.

And we're going to find out what.

(…which annoyed them a lot.)

More importantly, Harry wasn't bothered by the fact that he hadn't grown a millimetre. With only four days to go before the championship, he was still only 1.3 metres tall.

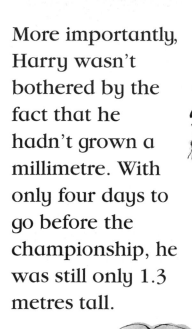

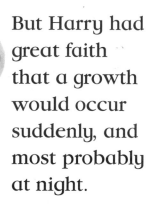

But Harry had great faith that a growth would occur suddenly, and most probably at night.

Hiding his extra training from his parents was another matter…

Chapter 6

On Friday night as he crept out to the
garage, Harry had no idea he was being
watched.

He settled himself into his usual position and hung there, thinking about his big ambition...

...for about ten seconds...

…when, suddenly, his peace was shattered.

You're not still trying to make the high jump team, are you, Fly?

Well, here, let's give you a helping hand.

Chapter 7

Next morning, Lucy took Harry to
The Gap for a pep-talk.

I'm no good
at anything.

That's
not true,
Harry.

Then how
come I even have to
get rescued by a girl? And
one who's taller than
me? I'm a joke.

"I can't believe they took the ladder. If I hadn't come along you might still be there now!" Lucy giggled.

But she stopped when she saw the expression on Harry's face. "You're brilliant at skimming stones!" she said.

"Great!' snapped Harry. "I'm brilliant at something completely useless!"

> You're running faster and springing higher...

> But not growing a billimetre!

Things didn't get any better for Harry. That night, when he measured himself…

One millimetre shorter! I've SHRUNK!!!

On Sunday morning he gave up any thought of training and stayed in bed.

When the phone rang downstairs, he pretended not to hear it.

When Lucy called round for him, he dived under the bedclothes and hid. As far as he was concerned, he was never leaving the house again.

Harry barely touched his Sunday lunch.
And he did his best to blot out what his
parents were saying…

Look! We've been making you a special banner.

HARRY FLY JUNIOR WE'RE SO PROUD OF YOU!

Can't wait to see you beat the pants off the opposition, son!

...when suddenly the realisation struck him.

41

For three weeks he had been hanging
from his arms, with the weights attached
to his feet. And his arms had got stronger.

Harry looked at his arms. Yes, they were
definitely stronger. And *longer*, too.
A centimetre longer – maybe more!

But his legs… there was no change at
all! Still as weedy and short as ever!

There was no time to lose!

That's our boy! Always raring to go!

Chapter 8

Harry couldn't believe how stupid he'd been. Of course! To stretch his legs, he should have been hanging *upside-down*!

"Every minute counts," Harry said to himself.

Minutes are millimetres, and millimetres will get me into the team!

Harry spent
every spare
minute hanging
upside-down.

He's
fanatic...
obsessed...
deluded!

Lucy worried about him.
Hanging upside-down as much as Harry
did couldn't be good for anyone. Thank
goodness the championship was only
two days away. The trouble was, she
was pretty certain that Harry wouldn't
be competing.

Harry thrust his arm
into the air and a
mighty roar filled
the stadium.

Harry nodded to the judge.
The crowd fell silent.

Harry ran towards
the high jump bar…

But with every
step he took
he shrank
smaller.

The harder he ran, the smaller he shrank!

By the time he reached the crash mat,
Harry was no bigger than an ant!

Again the crowd roared, but
not *for* him – *at* him.

Harry sat up, gasping for air. What a nightmare!

The numbers on his clock glowed 4:13, then flipped to 4:14.

In six hours he had to prove to Mr Stebbings that he should be in the team. Only six hours…

"Minutes are millimetres," whispered Harry, dragging himself out of bed.

Chapter 9

When the time for The Last Chance came, everyone wanted to see what would happen – even the teachers. Harry tried to ignore them as he walked on to the sports' field.

Are you really sure you want to do this again, Fly?

Yes, Sir.

Harry caught sight of Lucy. She nodded to him. *You can do it!*

And Harry ran...

Harry didn't open his eyes. He didn't need to. He knew it was all over.

Mr Stebbings patted his shoulder.

You did your best, Fly. There's always next year...

Even as he walked back across the field, Harry could hear the laughter.

Ha! Ha! Ha!

But he didn't care. There was only one thing on his mind.

How am I ever going to tell Mum and Dad?

Chapter 10

When Harry reached the classroom,
almost everyone started chanting.
Then he saw the ruler...

Gradually, the class pushed Harry closer to the ruler.

It was the last straw! All those weeks of training and hoping – and now this!

Tearing himself free, Harry grabbed the ruler with both hands and made a run for the door.

The window at the far end of the corridor was open. Gasping with rage, Harry ran towards it, the ruler still in his hand.

With every last bit of his strength, he hurled the ruler out of the window…

The ruler flew like an arrow

– over Mr Stebbings' head – over the school fence and

– over the graveyard
(narrowly missing the
church steeple)…

the houses beyond

...landing, finally, plum in the middle of Harry's own back garden.

Chapter 11

Back at school, everyone stood open-mouthed in awe. Then Lucy broke the silence.

By the time Mr Stebbings reached Harry
he was breathless,
but he was
smiling.

Will you throw
for us in the inter-
schools championship
tomorrow?

Umm...YES!

And when Mr and Mrs Fly heard the whole story, they were amazed.